Stephen Mellor

Stephen Mellor was born in Buchanan, Liberia, grew up in Yorkshire and
lives in Sheffield with his partner, and Moose, the excitable greyhound.
He is the creator and co-host of the podcast, Prompety Prompt.
Pyre is his first published work and was shortlisted for the 2022 Reflex Press
Novella Award.
His first novel, From Where We Threw Dogs, is due to be published shortly.

www.stephenmellor.net
twitter @sgmellorwriter
instagram stephenmellorwriter

'Pyre has a raw sensitivity that immediately catches the imagination. It's like
glimpsing something dark moving behind a fence: you keep thinking about
it, wondering what it was, and it slowly seeps into your dream.'
Eleonora Mignoli

Pyre

Stephen Mellor

For Alex, Harriet, and Gill

It's good to know something at the start

'I'm not naive.

I know what will happen,

I do.

I'm not blind to it.

But it doesn't stop me wishing —

Wishing I could have stopped you.

Wishing I could have stopped it all.'

Autumn

ONE

Life is full of simple decisions.

Or it is if you allow it to be.

Do you enjoy your meat clean, or do you devour anything? Like Pork. Pork is not clean. Pork is like us, stuffed full of all the shit on offer because a pig does not know when it is sated. And that's not all we share. We burn like pork. Not as in a roast conducted on a spit, where the heat is controlled, and the cook managed, and there is no chaos. Think instead of being consumed — consumed by a pyre.

If you want your meat clean, burn a lamb or a cow. You might not like the smell of either but at least you won't recognise your perfume within the roast. But, if you want to taste sin, like it is a long-lost friend, then burn a pig. Or even better, burn a body: because even if you were the cleanest living person since Joseph, in a pyre, your flesh will still squeal like a pig. Even the most sinless spit fat through the orifices gouged by the flames. You don't think of that; of how fire exposes every weakness there is in the flesh, or how the flames, that consume even the most innocent, turn the strongest stomachs because all that is body and thought and emotion melts off the bone like candle wax. And, as you stand witness to the skeleton rushing to become ash, you will never know innocence again.

By then you have shed your sensibilities. You have thrown them into the flames like cheap fuel into a winter's hearth. You have rejoiced as they mingle with the dust and all that is left once everything has cooled and crumbled. First to white, that enticing grey-white that deceives you into thinking it is clean and ready, even eager for your touch, and then to black.

And then to become, as all things become once the furnace has simmered to its boredom, no more no less than earth.

Jenny could have argued why it happened the first time —

Because she was alone and frightened and knew what she could lose.

And the second —

At a push.

But the third? Perhaps we would all grow accustomed to the worst of life if it is allowed to become a habit, or a process. A necessity for survival? Perhaps we are all capable of embracing the very worst of ourselves when the choice is as simple as us or them. But by the fourth time, there are no excuses. By the fifth there is no defence. Not in court. Not in the streets or markets, not in the pubs, or in the thoughts of the small minded souls who won't even recognise they sin with greater regularity because —

It is best you breath now. Sip your coffee, or whatever it is you're drinking. Her name is Jennifer by the way, she likes to be called Jenny. She doesn't like Jennifer.

I always call her Jennifer.

TWO

'Blood is always thicker than water,' Jenny's father told her when she was still young.

He told me, too.

Jenny knew what her father was wanting to tell her. She knew also what he was secretly telling her, but what he did not tell her was whose blood? Or what's blood? Or that sometimes, death comes without blood being shed. All Jenny knew was that blood is as much fuel to the fire as it is for life. When it is time, you take the blood from the life and you give it to the fire, but without it, everything dies.

So, Jenny burns sheep.

She burns sheep — and other animals.

THREE

It started with her father, and he started by doing a fellow farmer a favour. Before long he was burning the dead livestock for many other farmers during the first Foot and Mouth outbreak. You weren't supposed to do it, not at least until permission was given and then you had to be observed by an inspector. But sometimes the farmers don't want to wait for that. Or pay for it. Sometimes you just don't want the inspector, or anyone, to know there was death on your farm, not least because there's always death on a farm. As Jenny's father always said, 'Well, they'll only burn the poor buggers anyway. May as well do it our'sen.'

Except Foot and Mouth did not come. Not to what are now Jenny's fields, or any of the fields round here, at least not in the flesh. But it did come in reputation, and it did come in fear and no small dose of expectation.

It was like the inspectors wanted Foot and Mouth to be found, even if it wasn't there, and if anything died on a farm back then, they wanted to know why. They wanted to see the beast. They wanted to inspect it. They would swarm over you and your neighbours, even it if was not there to be found.

There was some compensation if your herd was lost, but you could make more if there were no doubts over the health of your animals. Quietly losing the odd beast here and there and slipping Jenny's father something for disposing of it was money well spent.

When, thirty years later, the disease came back, he was still doing it, and this time Jenny was helping him.

Now there's no Foot and Mouth, but animals still die, and they still bring them to Jenny.

In winter, when the winds do more than you can believe, when they spit and sting and strip the weak from the flocks, Jenny builds a pyre on the hill overlooking the meadow — the great natural amphitheatre that gapes into sight halfway along the track. If it's spring or summer, if it's good weather, she builds the pyre further away, over the brow and into the valley behind. Nobody walks there and everything is less visible. There's always wandering fools with curious eyes and wagging tongues and bleeding hearts. Those people don't understand, it makes no difference to the people who work these lands, a carcass is just a carcass. They should let death be death.

Jenny calls them, 'stupid fuckers'.

I best warn you. I don't like it when Jennifer swears. I know it's hypocritical, but she should do as I say, not as I do. But she's right. They are "stupid fuckers"'.

And blood does not flow in winter. Not like you think. It needs the heat of the fire — a fire to keep its flow, otherwise it freezes or becomes diseased by whatever is carried upon the wind. The wind here isn't some benevolent spirit that blows leaves around, maybe topples a rubbish bin or two when it's having a strop. It doesn't even cleanse. It is a devil.

And yes, you don't have to burn them. You could put the carcasses in the ground, but something would dig them up. You might say, 'But isn't that nature? The food chain? Life? But people like Jenny know better. Leave the scavengers a meal of the dead and the living will be next.

That's why the farmers first gave her father and now give Jenny the carcasses.

Because Jenny burns them.

She burns them good.

FOUR

Jenny was waiting in the yard, hair tied back in a scruffy ponytail, the odd wisp escaping the side, a cup of tea in one hand and the other in a pocket. It was a working day. Her overalls were her favourite. Blue and too big, turned over at the wrists and tucked into her dark green wellington boots.

Normally it is only her here, and two working sheepdogs, sisters, Meg and Jess, and Lord knows how many sheep. Jenny loves her herd, she loves her dogs, and she loves to see the kingfisher in the stream running beside the meadow, but some days Jenny doesn't want to be here.

She was waiting in the yard for Malcolm, an old friend of her father.

Have I told you her father is dead? I can't remember — but he is.

And so is her mother. Mother went first. Cancer. Father went soon after. Heart.

There is no need for sentimentality. It happens, and it happened some time ago. They used to run the farm together. Husband and wife, and then husband and wife and children.

Now it is just Jenny. There was a sister, but the sister went away. Went to America with some man from Leeds.

Malcolm arrived.

He said, 'I worry about you, lass' as Jenny bumped and manoeuvred her Defender over the tracks to the meadow and off onto the hill. Jenny didn't say anything back. The pyre was there, as she said it would be, away from prying eyes and inspectors and taxes.

Here they call each other *lad* or *lass*, until you reach a certain age, not that anyone knows what that age is. It depends on the individual. How they look, how they act, how they dress. Or if you're a woman, then they will use your Christian name, but you have to be married before that happens. Until then, like Jenny is now, you're still lass, and Malcolm is Malcolm, because he was a friend of her fathers, and his wife is Wendy. It has always been that way and no one here wants it to change.

Jenny didn't say anything back.

'It can't be easy?' Malcolm tried drawing her into conversation.

She didn't say anything back.

'You don't say much.'

She didn't say anything back.

As the sheep carcass Malcolm had brought with him burned, he said, again, 'It can't be easy, running all this by ye'sen?'

'You manage it.'

'But I'm not by me'sen. I have Wendy.'

Jenny didn't say anything back.

Malcolm said, 'Your fatha was always worried about you.'

'I were always worried about him, the amount he drank and smoked.'

'He wondered when you'd find time to marry.'

She didn't say anything back.

She didn't say anything back, not then, not on the way back down to the yard, not until she got out of the Defender. A proper Defender, mind; none of this city make up, just a filthy, old, rattling workhorse of a machine, stinking of livestock. Everyone had one. They all looked the same, they all smelled the same but somehow were different. They were all loved. All treated like part of the family. Then Jenny said, although she said it without ever looking at Malcolm, 'You don't have to worry. When there's someone worth marrying, I'll find the time.'

'Why don't you join me and Wendy for a drink tonight? Let us buy you supper at The Rose?'

'No.' She noted his hurt. 'No, thank you. It's kind of you, but — you know.'

'You can't avoid him forever. He's gonna be landlord there for quite a while.'

'That may be, but I can avoid him as long as I want to.'

'Well, if you change your mind, we'll be there for 'arf seven. Rains are comin' in. It's comin' hard. Don't be by ye'sen every night.'

Jenny thought Malcolm was sweet, always had been. Old fashioned but gentle, and well-meaning with it because whether Malcolm knew any different, he still let Jenny use the landlord as the excuse when it wasn't the landlord she was avoiding.

FIVE

Jenny's farm is the only one on the track. Nothing else except for the cottage when you first turn off the road through the village but nothing from there until the farm. The village is somewhere you pass though without noticing. There's not much here. Nine homes, that's all — nine homes and an old humped bridge which squeezes the road. Not that it was worth squeezing. In most places through the village the road is just a single track of tarmac, but at least there's tarmac.

Scattered around the bridge are the homes, and on the north side of the bridge is a three-way crossroad and the track to Jenny's farm, a rutted long established two-tyre track running a mile and a half from the bridge to the farm, a mile and a half of clippings and stone or mud and puddles with an overgrowing grassy line along its middle.

The brook that runs through the village and under the humped bridge is called the Burn by the villagers. It starts way off beyond Jenny's farm and runs alongside the track all the way to the village and through the village before disappearing out to the east.

It's meant to be full of otters.

Not that anyone has ever seen an otter in there.

Herons, yes, some fish, a family of kingfishers

But no otters. And no one knows why it's meant to have otters.

There is also a bus stop. It's next to the bridge and gets visited twice a day. Except on Sundays — when no bus comes.

When no one comes.

In the village, there are three farms, including Jenny's, with three families of farmers, four converted barns, two cottages, and a derelict old Georgian house which used to belong to the Skipton magistrate, although Jenny has never known why. Skipton's fifteen miles away, it's more than a half hour drive. Back then it would have been a half day ride. Some days —

Snow days, heavy rain days,

— it may as well be the other side of the world.

Not much has changed in Jenny's thirty-five years in and around these fields. The weeds have grown longer at the magistrate's house, a few of the windows have somehow been put through. A couple of the barns got converted, and they stopped doing livestock at the McGuire's. They just keep horses now. And old Mrs Jones died. She was always nice to

Jenny, and for as long as Jenny knew her, she lived alone. She had these strange sculptured heads on top of her gate posts. One day some walker passing through stopped and had a good look at them. Turned out they were Roman, two thousand years old, give or take. They're now in a museum on Hadrian's Wall. After she died, the cottage was sold to someone from Skipton, who lets it to strangers some weekends but most of the time it stands empty.

As for the sheep, Jenny was eight. She remembers her father sending her after school. He said, 'Stop off at Old Joseph's. He'll have an envelope for you. Ask the bus driver nicely, he'll hold the bus for a couple of minutes. You'll have to run, but it's do-able.'

And it was, not least because when Jenny was eight she was as frightened of her father as she was of God, especially when he said things like that to her, when he gave her such jobs.

Old Joseph's was in the village next on from Jenny's, four miles away and a metropolis by comparison, with its forty houses, a village green, a cricket team, three farm shops, a pub — The Rose, and a post box with a daily collection.

So, Jenny asked nicely and the bus driver took pity.

'Only two minutes mind' he said.

Off she set and was without breath or composure when she got to Old Joseph's door. He laughed, said, 'Been runnin' 'ave you, lass. 'Ere, take this for ya fatha, and be quick. There's a bit more in there than we sed. Tell 'im I'll be droppin' another round t'moro. Ground should be 'aard enuff to get Defenda reet up 'ill.' Old Joseph wasn't old at all, except to young Jenny.

The bus had waited. It had been waiting for more than two minutes. Jenny had run so hard she thought her lungs were about to burst.

The next village on from there was where Jenny went to school. Mr Longbottom had been the headteacher for what seemed like forever. When she was younger, through a heavy veil of tears, red cheeks and snatched breaths, Jenny had threatened — 'My fatha will come an' beat you up' — all because Mr Longbottom tried to get Jenny to eat broccoli. Her father never did punch him, but he did come and pick her up early. Jenny still doesn't eat broccoli.

Old Joseph died a few years back now. His farm passed, as they do round here, to his son, Peter. Peter is the same age as Jenny. They were in the same class at school all the way through from nursery. Jenny likes Peter. She liked his father, but she likes Peter more because out of all the boys she went to school with Peter never tried to touch her.

Jenny never knew how much was in that envelope but her father had said, 'When I'm gone, don't forget to put price up, and do it quick. They won't try and haggle with you whilst I'm still just a little bit warm.' He told her it kept the farm going. He wasn't wrong.

Before Jenny was ten she'd lost count of the number of carcasses she'd helped him cremate. Some were theirs, many weren't. Each time there was either an envelope or a handshake. Sometimes her father told her not to tell her mother they had done so many. He'd say, 'Don't go tellin' her. If we keep it secret, I get to surprise her with summut nice when we next go into Skipton.' Jenny always did keep it a secret because that way she got a treat too.

SIX

The nights can be bright with stars here.

It's because *here* is so far from anywhere, including any light pollution. You might get some at Keighley, or a little at Skipton but the village has only two streetlights and they struggle to illuminate anything other than themselves. One stands each side of the bridge and there's darkness all the way in-between. Everywhere else in the village and out to the farm, you can lie on your back at night and trace whatever constellation you dream of before letting the stars and the moon guide you home.

Not that night though.

Malcolm had been right. The rain had come in hard. A dense layer of vicious, moody low cloud dropped its unforgiving rain with a vengeance with which no windscreen could cope. He was also right in that it was not a night to be alone. When winter truly sets in there'd be plenty of nights spent alone with the dogs. Best get out whilst you can.

Jenny changed out of her farm clothes, threw on some jeans and boots and a jumper with a t-shirt beneath, pulled back her hair into a ponytail, the odd wisp escaping the side, applied a little lipstick and grabbed her phone, purse and more than a sensible dose of anxiety. She left the dogs with their supper and instructions to 'be good', threw a coat over her head and made a dash for the Defender.

It pays to know the roads round here, and it especially pays to know them on nights like that. It pays not to be drawn into some stupor by the dark and the dull rhythm of the wipers. It pays to keep scanning the brief view of the way ahead as a wiper passed by. It pays to watch for headlights approaching along with dips and twists. It pays to know when you could run wide and it pays to know where the flooded fall-always are and where the hedgerows loom like the devil — but Jenny didn't do any of this, not on the way back.

She did it on the way there.

But not on the way back.

She didn't do it on the way back because Jenny had had a drink. She had had more than one drink, and she was crying, crying as she drove, crying and angry because she had argued with Rosie and Rosie's husband —

The landlord

And Jenny had taken the long way home, along roads she didn't know quite as well and that's why Jenny hit her.

'I didn't see her. I didn't.'

I know. She must have run from one of the fields.

'She must have run through one of the side gates, out of one of the fields'

If the field is arable the side gates can often get left open and especially on nights like this because you know the weather is going to stop anyone going in the field. It's what happens, the gates get left open. She must have run out of one.

'I just didn't see her. I'm certain I didn't see her.'

You can't have seen her.

'I didn't even get chance to brake.'

And if you had seen her you would have stamped on the brakes.

'I just didn't see her. One moment the road was clear, the next she was there.'

Like an apparition in the headlights. So white and sudden and scared.

Then what happened?

'I smashed into her from behind.'

Did she go over the top?

'No, she went underneath.'

Is that all you remember?

'I remember her face.'

Her face? I thought you said you hit her from behind?

'I don't know, perhaps I did, perhaps I didn't, perhaps she twisted but that's what I remember.'

And nothing else?

'No.'

Not her hair?

Jenny shook her head.

What she was wearing?

Jenny shook her head.

Just her face?

All intensity and sodium as if captured by a camera flash. And her staring terrified eyes, and her mouth caught in a scream before she was gone. Disappeared into the dark and rain behind.

'I don't know, I don't remember.'

It could have been a dream? You could have hit a fox or something?

'No, I hit… I hit something. And I screamed. And I swore. I called her all sorts of names. I hit her.'

You don't do any of that in a dream.

Dreams keep you within by regulating your responses.

Anything extreme you break the boundaries —

Jenny had skidded the Defender to a halt.

'I don't remember doing that either, but that I must have done.'

Then what did you do?

'I just sat there. Gripping the steering wheel. My knuckles straining against the stretched white skin, thinking maybe it was a deer, or a sheep. Maybe a badger? No, not a badger; a badger isn't tall enough. It had to be a deer. Please, Lord, let it be a deer.

SEVEN

By the time Jenny had got out of the Defender and ran back up the road, ran back through the rain with her stride out of time with the rhythm of the hazard warning lights, she was breathless, she was soaked, and she was unsure of everything.

Everything.

Stay back. Let me deal with it.

'Are they okay?' Shouted Jenny. 'They just run out into the road. I couldn't stop. They just run out. Is she?'

I don't know, she's not moving. I'm trying to find a pulse.

'She just ran out.'

I heard you the first time.

'But she did. Is she?'

What?

'You know.'

I don't know. I can't find a pulse.

'She just ran out.'

I know

'I didn't mean to hit her. She just ran out. Oh God, I've killed her, haven't I?'

You're in shock.

'I didn't mean to.'

I need you to take a deep breath. I need you to calm down, and then stay calm.

'What do you mean, calm down? I've just killed someone.'

Sit down, will you. Just sit down. Let me see what I can do.

'You don't calm down after that. I've got to phone the police.'

Jenny took the phone out of her jacket pocket.

Wait.

'Fuck. There's no signal. There's no fucking signal. I need to get help. I should stay with the body.'

Just wait, will you. Think it through. You need to think it through.

'What?'

You need to think it through. Think. Where were you tonight?

'The Rose.'

And then where?

'Nowhere.'

Are you sure? Because you left The Rose a good while back. And you weren't in there that long, just long enough to get angry and knock a few back.

'No more than normal.'

Yes, more than normal. And everyone saw you, and everyone heard you, and everyone knew when you left.

'What do you mean, heard me?'

Everyone heard you. Your fight with the landlord.

'He was trying to charge me for something I didn't have.'

You threw your drink over him.

'Wendy and Malcolm weren't there. They'd already gone by the time I got there. They hadn't stopped. I was late, they thought I wasn't coming, what with the weather. He said I'd cost him two meals. Said they would have had the special. He said I had to pay.'

He was being a dick, but you could have just said no. You could have laughed at him. He wasn't serious.

'He wouldn't let me and Rosie chat. The fucking place wasn't even busy. And they had a waitress on. I just wanted to chat to Rosie, the fucking place wasn't even busy. I've got to phone the police.'

Don't you get it?

'Get what? I've got to phone the police.'

She's dead. Listen to me. Jennifer, I can't find a pulse. She's not breathing, she's not responding.

Jenny did not know what to say. She pointed down the road, then towards the hedgerow and then back to the body in the road.

'Rosie told me to leave.'

You don't need to phone the police or an ambulance.

'Rosie threw me out. She threw me out.'

You don't need to phone the police.

'I don't know what you're saying?'

Apart for you and me, there's no one about. If anyone else were around they would be here by now, but we're in the middle of nowhere, and it's late.

'I don't understand,' said Jenny, again, checking her phone for a signal. 'I need to phone the police.'

No, you don't.

Jenny didn't know what to say. She again pointed to the body, down the road, to the hedgerow, to the body.

You could just drive away. No one knows. No one ever has to know.

'What are you saying?'

You've had a drink tonight?

Jenny felt herself unable to speak.

You have, haven't you?

'They didn't have the wine I like.'

That doesn't matter.

'I was drinking gin instead.'

It doesn't matter.

'I shouldn't drink gin.'

If you call the police, it will be drink driving as well and not showing sufficient care. Don't look like that, it always is when you hit someone in the road.

'She ran out in front of me.'

And they'll be able to use the marks on the road where you skidded to work out how fast you were going. This won't be an accident. This will be manslaughter.

'But we can't just leave her here?'

I didn't say that.

'We have to go to the police. It was an accident.'

You've been drinking. They're not going to see this as an accident. No one is going to see this as an accident. A stormy night, you've had more than you should have had to drink — you were seen drinking. You had an argument with the landlord. You threw some bloke's full pint of beer over him. There are marks all over the road.

'But they'll believe me…'

Why would they?

'Because it's the truth?'

The truth is you had a drink, you were driving home and you hit her.

'She ran out. I didn't see her.'

You work the farm alone?

'So?'

So, who is going to work the farm for you when you're not there?

'What do you mean, not there? Where am I going to be?'

Where do you think? It's obvious. How many times do I have to remind you? You've been drinking.

'I only had the one.'

We both know that isn't true.

'They didn't have the wine I like.'

It doesn't matter.

'He knows I like that wine. They always have that wine in. It was an accident.'

Deny it all you like but think about it. We both know it's the only outcome from this, if you go to the police.

'Why are you helping me? She's dead.'

I don't know. Maybe it's because it could happen to anyone. Maybe it's because the landlord was a wanker to you. Maybe because they'll ask me where I was as well. Look, the body needs moving. It can't stay here, and it can't go in the back of the Defender. It will have marks from the impact, we can't add to that with anything to do with her. You got a van or something like that?

Jenny nodded. She mumbled, 'I've got a van.'

Then we go back to your farm and get the van.

'Yeah, yeah, we'll get the van.'

Then I'll come back and get her. If the worse comes to worse, I can say I found her lying in the road.

'What are you going to do with her?'

I don't know. I'll come up with something.

EIGHT

The knock on the door next morning sounded like the wind rattling a loose-fitting gate. It was as unexpected as expected. Jenny spilled the coffee she was cradling so tight, too tight,

'Shit.'

She said, more than once and the dogs scurried from around her ankles to their beds.

Still struggling, still disbelieving, still not expecting anyone but still expecting someone, everyone, to come to the farm, she let the damp heat of the coffee seep through the denim of her jeans.

'Shit, shit, shit. Shit. Who is it?' she called.

Me.

She didn't recognise the voice. She did recognise the voice. She didn't want to recognise the voice. She didn't — but she did.

Oh fuck,

She thought.

Oh fuck, but she shouted back —

'I'm coming'

— and crashed the mug on the wooden kitchen table. She didn't know why, why she spilled the coffee, why she was cradling it so tight, too tight, or why she shouted, again — 'I'm coming.'

Had she slept? Had she eaten? Had she even moved from the kitchen? She had vomited — more than once. She looked at the coffee spilling over the edge of what city folk would call a farmhouse-style table. She calls it the kitchen table. She remembered the night before.

'Give me a moment.'

Lingering with her hand near the spillage, thinking she might just wipe the coffee off the tabletop onto the floor. But she didn't. Instead, she checked her face and hair in the mirror hanging above the shoe rack which sits partly on the thread bare rug worn down from generations of boots traipsing along the hall from the farmyard door to the warmth of the kitchen with its stove and fireplace. She calls it a hall. It's not a hall. It's more like a corridor. She doesn't call it a corridor. Jenny doesn't know what it should be called.

Why, she thinks to herself, why check her hair?

What does it matter?

Because it matters. Everything matters.

Everything matters today.

She sends the dogs back to the kitchen. They wait in the doorway. 'Sit' she tells them. They sit. 'Stay.' And she opens the door.

It catches on the bristles of the door mat. She scolds herself, this time for not getting it sorted. She's been meaning to get it sorted for months. She thinks, I must get a different mat. They sell them in the market, in Skipton, every Tuesday and Thursday. I just need to remember, remember to go, remember to remember that when I do go, I need a new mat for the door.

Christ. Look at you. Didn't you sleep?

Jenny just stared, thinking fuck you. Fuck you, fuck you. Of course I didn't sleep. How could I sleep? How could anyone sleep after what happened last night? I should never have left. I should have stayed. I should have rung the police. It was someone's daughter, maybe someone's sister. Fuck, what if it was somebody's mother? Please God, not someone's mother.

Got to be calm. Fuck, how hard is it to be calm? I've got coffee on my jeans. What are you saying? Why are you so calm? Stop, stop talking. Stop walking away, I can't hear you.

Where are you going? Why are you waving? You waving at me? Why? To follow? I need to follow you? Is that the van? Why have they bought the van to the farm? Why park it there? Right in the middle of the yard? Anyone can see it. Who's going to see it? Only those who come down the lane to the farm. Fuck. Fuck. Fuck. It's worse than ever. Fuck, no.

Now, don't overreact.

What do you mean, don't overreact? I killed someone last night. How can anything I do today not be an overreaction? Why are you unlocking the van? Please say you don't, please say, please say you don't. Please say she's not in the back of the van? Don't unlock the van.

Don't open the doors.

Shit, thought Jenny, those doors squeak. You need some lubricant on those hinges. They sound like they've never had anything on them, they sound like they've not been opened in years. I've got some spray in with my tools, over in the barn, the old barn, that's where I keep, oh fuck, what's that?

'Is that her?' Jenny struggles to asks.

The back of the van is just the usual. Bare steel walls, with the rivets and the mouldings exposed for all to see. And a flat bedded floor, planked out with plywood, except for round the wheel arches. It's just like every transit van. Like every van ever, except for the bunched black tarpaulin. Bunched like she'd imagine it would be if there was a body wrapped inside.

You should burn her.

Jenny pictured a body in the tarpaulin. Trussed up like, like, like —

Did you hear me?

Jenny heard. She heard clear and crisp and clean as the wind sat high in the morning sky, having stripped the day clear of last night's storm to leave the sort of day you love, where you step outside the farmhouse door and take a deep breath and remember just how good this life can be, sometimes can be. When everything around you shouts of life and growth, and the dogs bound and cheer, excited for their work ahead. And the sheep are calm, and grazing and obedient and the crows on Crow Hill are settled and quiet. When the Burn is restful and the kingfisher tilts its rainbow head to the sun just like Jenny's doing now, or should be doing were it not for —

I asked if you heard me.

Of course, Jenny heard what was said. She heard it clear and crisp and clean. Heard every word, every fucking word.

You should burn the body.

When did it become a body?

Because it is.

When did it stop being a person?

It was a person, it was someone — it was.

Until last night.

It was a person.

It was a woman.

Until last night.

It was —

A mother

A sister

A daughter

She was someone.

Until last night.

Last night changed everything.

Yes, last night changed everything.

Now, she's a body.

Now, she's a body.

She won't even be that — if I'm going to burn her.

On the hillside, like I burn sheep, that's what's being suggested.

Turn around. That's what I should do, Jenny thought.

Turn around now. Walk back to the house. Lock the door. Call the police. Call someone.

Anyone.

Call everyone. Tell the world the truth.

Have you got something we can put her on?

Jenny couldn't think of anything to say. Instead, she just stared.

Stared, and refused to let herself think.

Like a tractor?

Yeah, yeah, I've got something. I've got the…the…that thing.'

Jenny couldn't think of its name just then, the name for the four-by-four chunky thing, big wheels, with a roll cage. Why did it have a roll cage? She didn't know.

Well, have you?

It came with it, the roll cage, it came with the vehicle when it arrived, like it came with a shovel, like a scoop on the front. And the scoop is the important thing because that's what Jenny uses to scoop up the sheep, the dead sheep, the dead anything, carcasses. That's what they are. They aren't anything else, just carcasses. Nothing breathing, nothing to personify, nothing to believe in, nothing to think of as anything other than the meat on their bones, nothing but a carcass and you carry them in the scoop, and because it's a four-wheel drive, it doesn't matter what the weather or the ground conditions, that thing goes anyway, any time, and if you have them in scoop, you just raise it up, over the pyre, you just raise it up and slightly tip it and off they roll into…

'Shit.'

I don't like you swearing.

'There isn't it…I've not built one.'

It was red — the scoop thing. It was red when Jenny bought it. It still is red. But bits of it are black, like the roll cage, and the seat. And the tyres.

'Wait here.' Jenny said.

She thought, did I just say that? Wait here? There's a body in the back of a van parked in the middle of the yard. Parked where anyone can see it. You don't want anyone waiting here. You don't want anyone.

What's got into me? Stop walking. Stop walking, don't get the keys to the shovel scoop thing, whatever its name is. Just don't.

NINE

I was beginning to think you'd run off.

'I had to get the keys. Besides, we can't just burn her. We need to burn her with something.'

Is that what the sheep is for?

'Yeah. We can put her underneath it. Help me get the sheep off and her in the scoop.'

It's a nifty little thing that. Is that what you call it, Scoop?

'What?'

Is that what you call it? Scoop?

It is now.

'Yeah.'

And how many dead sheep do you have lying around?

'I don't. That's why I was so long.'

You mean you just killed it. Wow, you're a hard woman. You killed it yourself?

'There's only me here.'

How?

'What does that matter? It's dead now.'

Aren't they expensive? Sheep?

Of course they're expensive, fucking expensive, thought Jenny. Like I wanted to kill it.

'Bolt gun.'

That's what you wanted to know, isn't it? I have a bolt gun back there. I don't like shot guns, but I have one. I just don't like to use it, so I have one of those instead.

'A bolt gun,' repeated Jenny.

That's the mark on its temple. It's a steel bolt that shoots into its skull, then recoils. Hate the thing, but it's better than anything else.

Do you need help? At the other end?

The other end? What are they talking about?

By the fire?

'Well, I've got to build the bloody thing first.'

Is that what the wood in the scoop is for?

'Yeah. Did you find anything?'

What do you mean?

'Last night. After you went back for the body. Did you find anything? Like why she was there? She wasn't dressed like a walker. Or a climber? So, why was she there?'

No. Nothing. Think she was lost.

'Lost? No one gets lost out there, not dressed the way she was.'

Skin-tight jeans and night-out sandals, a denim jacket and what looked like a spangly strappy top beneath.

Like I said. Nothing.

'Not even a purse, or a bag? A phone?'

God, please say there isn't a phone. They can trace phones, if it rings, or is turned on. Fuck. They can trace her phone.

No, nothing. No purse or phone, nothing. I looked. I did. I checked all up and down the road, and in the field next to the road. The gate was open though. I went back there first thing this morning as well. There's no way of tracing who she is, pretty sure of it. So, do you need my help or not?

'She's a student.'

What?

'She's a student.'

Jenny had pealed back the tarpaulin. She'd stared at the body and had begun to check through the clothes. In the front pocket of the jeans there was twenty-five pounds in cash. A ten and three fives, but no change, all notes. And a bank card and a student's union card that told everyone her name.

'She's a student.'

Was.

'What?'

Was. She was a student.

'Sorry,' Jenny said, not knowing why it was necessary to apologise. 'I know what her name…was.'

What was it?

'Do you really want to know?'

Yes.

'Amy. It was Amy. Amy Windle.'

Does it say where she was from?

'Lancaster Uni.'

Far enough away then. Good. That helps.

Her earrings were nice — Amy's earrings. Simple studs with sweet red stones. And she wore bangles around her wrists. Some string ones, like the travellers, Hindu style suggesting she had been abroad, long haul, as well as a bracelet from a high street jewellery chain. It had charms, two, three, four of them hanging off it. A dog, a ship, a turtle and a bottle, like a champagne bottle, probably from when she turned eighteen, she can't have been much older than that. Jenny liked the ship the most. She had always wanted to sail on one but never had. You can't get much further away from the sea than here.

Don't say her name.

'What?'

You were going to say her name. Don't keep saying her name.

'Why?'

Because it doesn't bring her back.

Jenny decided it didn't seem right to add these trinkets and belongings to the pyre. There should be something to remember Amy Windle by. There should be something that everyone is remembered by. No one should just slip off this earth and leave nothing, and she was someone after all. Jenny slipped the trinkets, the earrings, the cash, and the cards into her own pocket.

So, do you need my help?

'No. You go. I can do this alone.'

I do everything alone. I'm used to it.

TEN

Later, alone on the hillside, with the light beginning to fade, having stood beside the unlit pyre for some hours, Jenny waited until the fire burned so hot and so deep no-one could tell what was hidden in its heart.

ELEVEN

The farm has a cellar.

Jenny keeps things down there.

Things she doesn't need or want any more but help her remember in some manner, like old dolls, a teddy bear or two, the denim jacket from her teenage years, some photos of old school friends, some photos from country shows, but no photos of the ex-boyfriend. She doesn't want him down there; she doesn't want him anywhere.

And photos of me. A few of me.

They're all in an old photobook. Mainly stuck in, some loose because the glue's dried out — except for the strip of four pictures her and Rosie, taken in the passport photo booth on Skipton Station on their way to Leeds to be teenage rebels for the day. She always kept the strip loose. She used to like to take the strip of pictures out with her from time to time, usually on a sunny day when there was nothing for her to do. She'd go up on the hills above the meadow and lie in the long grass and look at them with a blue sky behind them. Pictures one and two were just her and Rosie, laughing, hugging, big hair, and bleached denim. In the third one they were pulling silly faces, and the final one, kissing. They were taken in the same photo booth where Jenny's first boyfriend, her only boyfriend, tried to touch her, grabbing her breasts and laughing as the flash went off. Bastard. He got a punch in the balls for his trouble, but he still behaved as if he was the winner. The winner of what, she never understood.

Jenny found an old coffee tin that held some random unmatched nails, many different sizes and lengths, some still smooth and unsullied, others looking older than her, some looked like they'd been yanked from some wood and were twisted or bent or squeezed at all different points on their length. She transferred them all to a larger tin of nails, and replaced them with Amy Windle's cash, her students union card, the studs and the bracelets. No need to hide the jar, just put it back on the same shelf, in the same place as it was before. No one comes down here, no one but Jenny and at least it will be something to remember Amy Windle by. Back upstairs night was falling. The sky was still clear, as if now celebratory, for either Amy Windle's life or Jenny's subterfuge - or both.

Winter

TWELVE

Winter here passes without comment. Mostly.

Heavy snow, when it comes, and it will come, means swollen rivers and flooded fields and we become invisible like we're somehow lost in the blizzard, a blizzard on their own lands. Can you imagine that?

No one visits.

No one comes.

No one calls in the farm shops for their virtuous take-on-your-way cheeses and meats and home-made marinaded cuts.

Instead, they wait.

They wait for the good weather, and whilst they wait, we farmers exist, as we always did — without. Without you. Without others, without anyone but ourselves. Why? Because it's easier that way.

We keep the livestock off the hills but still some are lost. It's inevitable, but saddening, even when it happens every year.

Spring will bring new life, it always does, and whilst we welcome it, we never take it for granted. We never trust its release from winter, always looking over our shoulders for the signs of late storms and snows. You don't. No, you don't, and you don't care. You just appear and frolic and traipse across our fields to swoon over the lambs you'll later devour in the pubs and hotels and then complain about the price in the supermarkets in the cities you so love.

Hello. Again.

'You?'

Yes.

'You again?'

Yes, me. Again.

Why, thought Jenny, why? She's gone? All of her It's over? No one has come looking for her. There's been nothing on the news. It's over?'

Thought I'd just pop in. Everything okay? Did you, you know, sort things?

'Yes,' said Jenny.

Good, because I was worried.

'She was a student.'

Who was?

'Amy Windle. She was a student.'

I know.

'Because you said before you didn't know her name or what she was.'

But you told me.

'Yes, I did. I remember. Because you didn't take the time to look in her pockets? I did. I found out her name. I can't find out anything else, not without people knowing. But I know her name, and that means she's someone. Was someone. And someone is going to want to know where she is? Is that what you're worried about?'

No. I was worried about you.

Why did you have to say that, thought Jenny, why? Are you reading my thoughts? I don't want you reading my thoughts. And I don't want you thinking about me. I don't want you worrying about me. You never used to before. I don't. I don't worry. I don't worry about me. I'm perfectly capable. I'm happy with my life. I know what I am. No one needs to tell me, or judge me, or search for pity, because I know what I am and who I am and I know what I've done, so, no, I don't need you, so, stop. And don't worry about me.

'I'm fine,' said Jenny.

Good, because it's been a while.

'It's been a few weeks.'

More than a few weeks.

'A month or two.'

'Three months I think.'

So why now? Why have you come back? Jenny didn't say that. She just nodded.

I guess you're wondering why I've come back?

Jenny just nodded.

I need your help. I had an accident. Bit like you did. I hit some ice. Lost control.

It is winter, was Jenny's first thought. All the sheep are down off the hills.

She said, 'Well, it is winter. Most of the roads round here never get treated — unless we do them.'

I hadn't been drinking, or anything, but it was dark. Well, nearly dark.

You don't mean it like that, do you? We're not talking about a scuff or a bump. You're talking about like before. Oh, please tell me there isn't a body in the back of the van.

There was a cyclist, coming the other way. Towards me. She didn't have any lights on.

So, there is? There's a body in the back of the van?

You can stop looking like that. It wasn't anywhere around here.

'It doesn't matter where it is. All the sheep are down in the lower fields. If it gets really cold we move them into the barns. No one is getting rid of sheep now.

It was over Huddersfield way.

Don't they treat the roads over there like we do, thought Jenny, not that we treat all of them, but people still have to get around and if we don't treat the roads, up here at least, then no one gets around.

I was going over the tops up there. It was dark.

Jenny wondered, why would anyone be out cycling in the dark, in winter, up over the tops. No, don't open the back of the van. I don't want to see what's in there. Don't open the doors, just turn around, get in the van, drive off, for fucks sake drive off. And I never want to say anything about it again, ever, you understand? Never. So turn around. Don't open the doors, oh fuck the doors are open. Will you not get them looked at? That squeaking, it just needs some spray on the joints, it's so fucking easy to do. It takes a second, I'll even get you my stuff, it's in the old barn over there, where I keep my tools and the bits and pieces I don't want anymore, don't need anymore, the stuff I hardly use…

'Morning Jenny.'

A familiar voice from over the far side of the yard, over by the gate, the open gate, the gate left open, the gate leading out on to the track to the village.

'Malcolm?'

Shouted Jenny.

'What are you doing here, Malcolm?'

It's Malcolm, Jenny's head reels. Here, in the yard, Malcolm.

You want me to close the van doors?

Yes, it's Malcolm. Close those doors.

Close the doors, what?

Close the fucking doors.

No.

Close the fucking doors, it's Malcolm.

Close the fucking doors, what?

Please.

That's all you had to say.

'Malcolm, hello.'

Jenny again shouted, this time in reply to nothing as Malcom approached across the yard. She stepped forward, away from the van, to meet him.

'How's you?' she said, 'How's Wendy?'

'She's very well, thank you. Actually, it's about Wendy I'm here. Not a bad time is it?'

'No. Er, just got… no.'

'I won't keep you. Just wanted to invite you to the Rose on Friday night, having a bit of a surprise get together for Wendy's birthday. Don't go tellin' her now will you. So far I've got away with it. That van's seen better days, hey, Jenny?'

'Always good to get away with something now and then, hey Malcolm.'

'Hah hah hah, exactly. So, you'll be there, about eight? No later, Wendy will be there about half past.'

'I'll do my best to be there,' Jenny said.

And Malcolm, knowing her well enough not to press further, gave her a quick hug and said his goodbyes adding, 'And this time don't let the weather put you off. It's going to be windy over the weekend but that's all,' before briskly walking back to the road, waving as he went.

You should go.

'It's none of your business.'

He's a gud'un that Malcolm. Always looking out for you. You should go. Don't look at me like that. It's a nice pub, The Rose. Full of friendly people. Malcolm and Wendy especially. They're lovely. Except the landlord, he's a twat. The landlady's nice too. But you already know that. And she likes you, even though you did throw that pint over her husband. But you also know that. In fact, I think she likes you a lot. What's her name? Rosie? Rosie of The Rose. I think that's funny. Good job she married into it, so to speak. Would have been a bit tragic if her parents had the pub before her and named her after it. Rosie of The Rose. You two go back a few years, don't you?

'I can't do anything with what's in the van.'

Yeah, yeah, I know. It's winter and the sheep are in the barns or whatever it was. No, none of that. You are going to help me. In fact, I'm sure of it.'

'Once was enough.'

No. Once was looking after you, which I did. Didn't have to. Could've gone to the police.

'I wanted to go to the police.'

Well, I didn't stop you. You stopped yourself. You knew what you'd lose if you did. Thing is, so did I, which is why I know you're now going to help me. So, let's get that tarpaulin out of this van and you can then fetch that scoop thing of yours.

Jenny returned with the scoop. Behind the closed back doors of the van the now familiar black slab of tarpaulin occupied the yard like the most grotesque delivery since the family of foxes attacked the lambs three springs ago. Shit, Jenny thought. Shit, shit, shit.

THIRTEEN

What Jenny had been told was the truth. Sort of. In the tarpaulin was a cyclist in the standard uniform of padded lycra shorts and a tight racing top adorned with the name of some cycling team. The cyclist's hands were still guarded by cycling gloves, but these were scuffed, and her shoes were missing. She had a phone in a strapping on her left upper arm, but it had been smashed beyond being saved, and there were no headphones. There was bruising about the face and neck and around the wrists there was no other sign of her having crashed off a bike. With the phone in the arm strapping was a key. A Yale key. A house key, together with one bank card slipped between the phone and its outer waterproof casing. Lucy Atkinson was her name, or at least the name on the card, and Lucy Atkinson was somewhere in her late twenties, Jenny guessed. She was pale skinned, though the broken blood vessels darkened her complexion. It was a ghoulish makeover all too Halloween for Jenny's taste.

Jenny kept the phone, bankcard, and another pair of plain stud earrings, together with the house key, and put them in another coffee jar on the same shelf as Amy Windle's. Except this time she added a piece of scrap paper scrawled with the date she believed the woman to have died. Later she went back through the diary and was able to isolate the date Amy Windle died. She wrote that on another piece of scrap paper and added it to Amy's jar.

Jenny slept better that night than she expected and next morning decided she would go to The Rose on Friday. She'd even wear lipstick and do something with her hair.

So, Rosie likes me?

It was a thought in which Jenny was able to lose herself, until she stepped out to the farmhouse and remembered what yesterday had been laid in the yard.

FOURTEEN

'I thought I'd told you. You're not welcome here anymore.'

It was Friday night.

'Malcolm invited me. He was insistent.'

Was he now?'

'Jenny, you made it,' said Rosie, pushing her husband, Tom, further along the bar at The Rose. 'Jack needs servin', so get ye'sen to it,' she said before turning back to Jenny. 'What have you been up to, your hair looks amazing.'

Jenny blushed.

Rosie hugged her.

She kissed both cheeks.

Jenny did not want to let go.

'Wow, Jenny, I've not seen you look as good as this since, well for months and months. Reminds me of that time we went to Leeds. You remember, don't you?'

Jenny nodded. 'I've still got those pictures of us from the booth at Skipton Station,' she said and was immediately gripped with a sudden fear that she had shared too much, too quick.

'You haven't? What, all of them?'

Jenny nodded.

Rosie blushed. She said, 'It was a good day, wasn't it? Remember those dresses we tried on in that posh shop?'

'You looked amazing in yours.' It was something Jenny could still remember in vivid detail, right down to Rosie's Doc Martin boots and the little flowers on her exposed bra strap.

'And you did too. Shame we could never have afforded them.'

'We'd have looked well out of place wearing them, with our wellies and.' Jenny didn't finish her sentence.

'But we would have had all the boys in Skipton chasing us. You here for Wendy's surprise party?'

'Yes. Malcolm came by the farm the other day. Surprised me. I thought he'd just ring up to ask.'

'They're worried about you.'

'Worried? Wendy and Malcolm? Why?'

'Rosie, are you going to help me at all tonight,' shouted Tom, as he pulled a pint and demanded 'anything else' off the customer.

'In a moment.' Rosie shouted back at her husband, before giggling more with Jenny and telling her to 'Ignore him.'

'I try hard to. What did you ever see in him?'

'A chance not to spend my life as a farmer's wife. Plus with a surname like his, I thought he was Italian. I thought he was going to whisk me off to Italy to live in the sun forever.'

'I thought his mum and dad were sausage makers?'

'Yeah, well I didn't know that. Not until it was too late. I was never like you, Jenny. Nowhere near as practical or as capable as you. At least, this way, I get to spend my time in here on nights like that storm. I loved it when you threw that pint over Tom. He was being such a wanker that night. I'd been trying all night to get across to talk to you but you left so early.'

'Why's Malcom worried? He's no need to be.'

Before Rosie could answer someone shouted, 'They're 'ere' and Jenny was shunted, along with everyone else, in front of the bar. When the door open, they all shouted 'Surprise.'

Wendy squealed and blushed and said something about nearly wetting herself, adding, 'Thank goodness for Tena Lady.' Everyone laughed and after she established it was all

Malcolm's doing, she gave him a full-on kiss with her hands planted firmly on his cheeks.

Someone shouted, 'Hey up, Malcolm, you'll be on a promise t'neet.'

Jenny watched Wendy working her way around the crowd of people in the pub, each one met with a smile, a giggle, some with a hug. When Wendy saw Jenny she called out, 'Oh, you made it. Wonderful, I was just asking about you, wasn't I, I was just asking about her, Malcolm, wasn't I.'

Jenny gave her a hug. 'Happy birthday, Wendy.'

'Thank you, dear, and all the better because you're here. We've been so worried about you.' Wendy took the bottle of wine and a glass being handed to her by Malcolm. 'And a glass for Jenny as well' she shouted at Malcolm who was heading back to the bar. 'It's from California so it must be good — or at least that's what Twat Face behind the bar says.'

Jenny smiled at Wendy's use of Twat Face, instead of Tom.

'I wish I knew why you and Tom don't get on,' said Wendy as she did nearly every time they met.

'Me too,' lied Jenny as she did every time Wendy asked her.

'Still, you're here and that's all that matter.'

Tom and Rosie had laid on some food and later in the evening Tom started up the disco, microphoning his way over the start and end of every record with some comment only he thought funny. Time to go, thought Jenny. Time to go.

Rosie was too busy serving behind the bar to say a proper goodbye so Jenny loitered for a while by the glass collecting point but all Rosie managed, much to Jenny's disappointment was a brief wave and a blown kiss. A quick goodnight to Wendy and Jenny was away. The night air was chilling. It was still too early in the year to be lingering outside without a coat.

You took your time.

Jenny recognised the voice. Turn away was her first thought. Turn away and keep walking, pretend you hadn't heard. Get in the Defender, lock the door, and go.

I know I said you should go but…

'But what?'

Did you have to be so long?

'Fuck off.'

There's no need for that, and you know I don't like you swearing.

'What do you want?'

I thought you'd be more pleased to see me. I was thinking that perhaps you and I could grab a coffee, seeing as we now have so much in common.

'We're not friends.'

Oh, you don't mean that.

'I think the less we see of each other, the better.'

I'm not a bad person. And don't forget I did you a favour. I got you out of a hole, remember?

'And I did the same for you, so let's call it even and leave it at that.'

So, it went okay then? Malcolm didn't come round again?

'Bloody good job he didn't. Don't ever do that again.'

I don't intend to make a habit of it. It was just an accident, that's all.

'She was somebody, you know.'

We are all somebody.

'She was somebody to someone.'

You don't know that. If she was somebody to someone she wouldn't have been cycling in the dark on the tops above Huddersfield, now would she?

'That's not how being somebody works.'

Stop being so precious. We're in this together, you and me and don't go forgetting that.

'That sounds like a threat.'

Well, I'm sure you wouldn't want your little girlfriend behind the bar in there finding out the truth, now would you. School friends, weren't you? Has she ever worked out you fancy her, or did you have a dabble when you were younger? Wonder how the village will react if they knew they had a pussy-licker amongst them. Doesn't strike me like the sort of place you'd want that reputation. So, how about that coffee sometime?

'The answer is still no.'

Oh, come on, stop playing so hard to get. I know a few of your sort. I could bring one round with me if you wanted. A pretty one. Maybe make a night of it.

'Is that what Lucy Atkinson was?'

Who?

'The girl on the bike.'

Oh, her. Yeah, no idea. I told you, she was an accident. Maybe the girl you ran over?

'Amy Windle.'

Yeah, her, maybe she was too. Or was that why she was running away? Is that why she was out there dressed like she was? Bit of an overreaction, wasn't it? Just because she wouldn't let you dip your fingers.

'Leave me alone.'

Or maybe I could ask your landlady friend in there if she fancies some fun. Hubby might be a tosser, but she's okay. I bet you'd go for that, even if he was part of the bargain as well.

'You come near me again and I'll run you down.'

I don't have to come near you. I'll just go and talk to the landlady.

'Don't you dare go near Rosie. Don't you dare.'

Or what? Thought so. I'll make you a deal. I'll not go and talk to Rosie if you put the kettle on tomorrow morning. A coffee and a couple of biscuits perhaps? You do have biscuits? Or shall I bring them? We could even take a walk. You could show me where you build the fires. I'd like that. I'd like to see what you did with them.

Jenny didn't want to agree. She didn't want her car door being held open, the frame being filled by this collision of memory, guilt, and fresh threat. So she said nothing. She just stared straight ahead.

Good, then it's agreed. I'll come round tomorrow. At eleven.

Jenny still said nothing.

I think the phrase you're looking for is, looking forward to it. I know I am. Drive home safely, won't you. Don't go hitting anything. Or anyone, I'd hate something like that to get in the way of our coffee.

'You know where I build the pyres.'

I know where you have built a pyre. It might have changed. So, coffee it is. Tomorrow.

'It's just a quick coffee.'

Whatever you say, Jenny. Whatever you say. I'll see you in the morning.

FIFTEEN

Do you have a fire ready?

It was next morning.

Jenny took a moment before answering. 'Why do you ask?'

Just curious.

Jenny took another moment.

'No.'

So, you build them specially?

Jenny nodded.

And does the size of the fire depend on the size of what you're burning?

Jenny nodded again.

You're not very talkative.

'Fuck you.'

Now, that's not very nice. But I imagine it's been a while for you. Don't look so disgusted. You really should have let me bring a friend.

'Never in a million years.'

Why don't you show me where you burn these sheep?

It wasn't even an attempt at irony.

Outside Jenny pointed to the Defender, and said, 'Get in.' It was hard to hear the instruction because the wind was strong, if not stronger than Malcolm had predicted.

They drove out the farmyard and bumped and rolled along the track to the meadow where, just a few feet inside the boundary, Jenny pulled up, knocked the Land Rover out of gear but left the engine running, and pointed to a patch of browned earth up to the far side of the banked hillside encircling the grassy flatland like the seating at a Roman theatre. Remnants of burnt wood were just visible in a sea of otherwise strong grass being sent berserk in the wind.

Nice. So that's how it ends up, just the scorched earth and some bits of brittle wood. It is wood?

'It's whatever's left. I scoop most of it up and throw it in with the pigs.'

I've heard pigs like that sort of stuff.

'They'll eat anything, whether they like it or not is a different question.'

How long do they take to build?

'A couple of hours. If you have the wood to hand.'

Have you got the wood to hand?

'Why?'

Just asking.

'You've got another body, haven't you?'

I'm just asking.

'I don't have the wood.'

Then it's a good job I don't have another body. What do you take me for? You think I go around running people over for fun? I'm just making conversation.

They sat in silence looking out over the meadow and up the hillside. The still idling engine kept the windscreen and windows from steaming up.

A sorry would be nice.

'For what?' said Jenny.

For thinking I had another body.

'Well, you've had two already, why wouldn't I worry you had another?'

That's not fair. One of those was your doing.

'How could I forget? You seem determined to never let me forget.'

You're a hard woman.

'You have to be out here.'

And death doesn't phase you?

'It comes with the land. You get used to dealing with it.'

The Defender shivered as the wind repeatedly charged against it.

What about that coffee then?

'If you insist.'

SIXTEEN

I love this picture.

Jenny's attention was dragged from making the coffee to the picture of her, her sister, and her parents framed on the kitchen wall. They were standing in a line and leaning forward on one of the gates to the meadow. Jenny was stood between her mother and her father, who was head and shoulders above them both, an arm around their shoulders. Her sister was leaning her head on their mother's shoulder.

How long has it been?

'Since they died?'

Since this picture.

'A few years.'

I would have thought more than a few. More like seven or eight?

Reluctantly, Jenny said, 'You're probably right.'

Something romantic about it, really. One going first and the other so soon after.

'There was nothing romantic about it. Dad's heart was clogged full of shit.'

And here you are now, running the farm, just like he always wanted.

'Someone had to keep it going.'

Why not sell it?

'And do what?'

Whatever you wanted.

'No one's buying farms now. At least not out here.'

Not even other farms?

'We're all up to our necks in debt.'

One bad winter away from disaster.

'One bad anything.'

And you get to make a bit on the side, getting rid of the dead animals for the other farmers.

'It's one of the reasons. But you know that as much as anyone. Nothing's changed in years. We're still the last farm in miles and inspectors still don't get out here much.'

And when they do?

'Then they rarely venture to the other meadows.'

What if someone tipped them off?

'Who would do that? I help all the farmers the same way. One goes down, we all go down.'

What if it wasn't a farmer?

'You threatening me again?'

Not me. Remember; one goes down, we both go down. I'm thinking more, I don't know, a pub landlord.

'He's doing too many dodgy deals himself. Besides he'd lose all his regulars.'

I got the impression he doesn't like his regulars.

'He doesn't. But he needs them.'

So, everyone is propping everyone up.

'You could say that.'

The coffee was served, as were five biscuits. Jenny chose them with care, ensuring they were the oldest and most stale. She didn't touch them.

Have you never fancied not having to do this anymore?

'You mean coffee with you?'

No. Farming.

'Every single day of my life.'

You hate it?

'No. I love it. Just don't want to do it anymore.'

How about I help you with that?

'I think you need to go now.'

I learned a few things while I've been away.

'You need to go.'

You should think about it.

'I've thought about it and the answer is still no.'

You didn't think for very long.

'Didn't need to.'

Very well. But we both know you need to a build a pyre.

'I'm not doing it,' said Jenny, before she had even realised what was being asked of her.

You will. Not least because it's really going to smell. It's been in there since last night. I'd say it's got twelve more hours before it starts to attract — attention. It's been nice chatting, Jennifer. Lovely coffee. Biscuits were a little stale. I'll bring my own next time. See you around.

The cold northern air swept into the kitchen. Jenny knew the farmhouse door was open and catching again on the mat. The doorknocker and letter box rattled. She heard the shout.

All yours, Jennifer —

Before it too was carried away into the wind.

She left it for a few minutes before going out into the yard. Another tarpaulin, secured with strong black tape, lay abandoned in the usual place. Jenny whistled the dogs back inside, turned around, and shut the door behind her.

SEVENTEEN

Jenny has a cold store.

An old-fashioned cold store out-house with thick insulating stone walls and thin slivers of light angled to pierce the darkest corners. A marble-topped plinth stands proud and unmovable, the centre piece above which a pulley hangs, rusted and stuck.

She would watch her father butcher many a pheasant, lamb, rabbit, and turkey on that altar. Jenny, however, had never used it. Time had changed the way lives are lived and without her father's insistence on keeping it scrubbed, a Sunday morning routine her older sister always talked herself out of, it became a place Jenny did not like to be. But now, it seemed the right place, the only place for storing death.

Using the scoop Jenny brought the tarpaulin from the yard to the cold store door. Using all her strength she freed the stuck mechanism which allowed her to manoeuvre the tarpaulin onto the tabletop. None of this felt spiritual, but somehow scientific, medical, suitable, private — even without a lock on the old wooden door.

Then, she went back to the meadow, counting on the earlier morning mist to keep the in-week ramblers away. Signs and warnings rarely did the trick, most seemed incapable of reading. Like all farms in the Dales Jenny's had allocated trails, with markings and gates that were easy to open and close, that tried to politely oblige their curiosity whilst channelling their direction. It didn't always work. Bad weather would keep them at bay; bad weather and a shot gun bent over an elbow. That often revived their reading abilities and put a swift skip into the strides back to the footpaths.

Jenny felt she had to hurry. Once built, the pyre stood a little over waist height. In the centre, surrounded and guarded by the outer higher walls of slatted wood, was a place of rest for the offering. The casual observer would struggle to see what was being burned. Only by standing close and peering over the sides would a body be discernible. When it came time, Jenny would add diesel to the fire to mask any human stench. She decided she was not going to waste another healthy sheep.

Back at the cold store the contents of the heavily taped tarpaulin intrigued Jenny.

In her heart she didn't want to be intrigued, but she was. Something was telling her to at least see the face. Jenny whispered, 'Before I send you on your way.'

Their way: she hadn't thought of it before and it was a shock to think of it now. She was their coroner, confessor, and gravedigger. She had the honour of ushering them from this life to the next. Hers was the last face this soul would see. Choosing the sharpest knife to hand, and with great care, she ran a thin slit through both the determined strapping and the tarpaulin, easing apart the plastic shroud to reveal the face. Deep down, Jenny knew what she was going to find.

'I should have guessed,' she said. 'It was never going to be a man.'

The woman was a brunette. Her eyes were swollen closed, but whether by death or beaten flesh, Jenny did not know. Her red lipstick was dry and patchy, but still strangely bright amongst the badly bruised face.

'Fucker' was all Jenny said as she slit the tarpaulin further open to find a torn blue blouse with all its buttons missing, revealing a black bra strap.

Jenny eased the shroud open further.

The body inside — the woman inside — was naked from the waist down. No shoes either.

Jenny rushed to the sink in the corner and vomited.

Vomited until her throat burned from the acids of an empty stomach.

One of the dogs came close. Jenny patted it and took comfort from its concerned eyes and tilted head.

'You'll keep me safe, won't you, Meg.'

There were no possessions on this woman that Jenny could use to identify her. Nothing to preserve as she had the previous bodies except for three rings. One of them obviously an engagement ring, the others looked old and Jenny thought they must have been passed down through the generations. She took these and snipped a few locks of the woman's hair to add to the memories. At least it was something. Jenny repackaged the shroud, and with all the solemnness she could manage whilst moving a body alone, she loaded the woman onto the scoop. Fifteen minutes later Jenny rolled the woman from the scoop into the open casket of the pyre.

In the loneliness of the Dales Jenny was always happier than anywhere she'd ever been, except for those brief moments in the photo booth on Skipton Station. Not that she'd experienced much other than that, unlike her sister who had sent postcards back from all over North America. Jenny said a prayer. 'Lord, forgive us. Forgive us both. Her and me.' It was all she could think was appropriate. Appropriate, and necessary.

Then Jenny lit the pyre, stepping back as the flames rose instantly.

Whatever her sins, Jenny didn't know those of the other woman, she just knew she had preserved her own life over another. Slumped on the wet grass and resting against the tyre of the Defender, she waited with the pyre. She waited, and she cried.

Spring

EIGHTEEN

The fourth body was five weeks after the third.

Despite the time of the year there was a strong frost on the ground. Footsteps crunched.

'What had you done to her?' said Jenny, quick and stern and impatient, her shotgun cradled across an arm.

Well, hello to you too.

'She was naked.'

Who was?

'The last — body. What are you doing to them?'

I'm doing nothing to them.

'She was beaten and naked from the waist down. What did you do to her?'

Nothing. Why do you insist on thinking the worst of me? I'm not a monster.

'I don't fucking believe you.'

Jenny's expression was both pained and full of anger.

You swear too much.

'Oh, do I?'

I don't like it when you swear.

'Well, tough fucking…fuck.'

Women should not swear.

'What are you, some fucked-up puritan? Is that why you're killing women? Fuck, am I next?'

If you want to mock me —

'I want to blow your fucking head off. I want you to never come here again.'

I reached out to you. I helped you.

'Don't you blame me for this.'

All I wanted was to help you.

'I didn't need your help.'

I stood up for you.

'I never wanted you to.'

They all said you couldn't keep the farm up. They said you couldn't do it alone. I wanted to help you. I still want to help you, despite how you treat me.

'I treat you? Fuck off. All you do is turn up with —' Jenny struggled to finish her sentence, because — 'You haven't? You fucking have.'

Stop swearing. I don't like it.

'No, I fucking won't. And what are you doing now? Are you five. Why have you got your hands over your ears?'

I don't like you swearing.

Jenny put her hands over her own ears to mimic and started to stomp around in a circle, screaming, 'Fuck, fuck, fuck, fuck fuck fuck.'

Suddenly aware of what she was doing and suddenly panicked and embarrassed and scared Jenny stopped and after catching her breath and composure said, 'What did you do to her?'

Stop swearing and I'll tell you.

'You'll tell me or I will fucking shoot you. As God is my witness, I'm past caring. Did you rape her?'

I didn't rape her. I wouldn't do that.

'So, what did you do. You got her drunk and fucked her?'

Stop swearing.

'What did you do to her?'

I just wanted to help you.

'I don't need your help.'

But they said you needed it.

'Who? Who said? Who have you been talking to?'

They worry about you.

'Who?'

Pause. There was a pause.

A long pause.

'Who?' Jenny repeated.

I just wanted to help you.

'Who?'

Jenny cocked the shotgun.

You would have lost the farm.

'Who?' Jenny aimed the barrel.

You don't need to do that.

'What did you do to her?'

You don't need to do that.

Their tone had shifted, no longer the accused, now a sudden supreme confidence.

'Don't I? Well, get this. I swear, I like women, I burn dead bodies. I'm not going to lose this farm. How's that for the start of a list? So, what are you going to do to me? Am I next in your sick reasoning? Am I Am I?'

You don't need to do that.

'I could blow your head right off. I could be free of you, right now, and no one else needs to die.'

You don't need to do that.'

'Stop saying that.'

But you don't. I'm not going to hurt you.

'Why should I believe you?'

I've told you before, we're together in this.

'Don't say that.'

But it's the truth. And that's what we deal in, you and I. We deal in the truth.

'I have no idea what you're talking about.'

You and I, Jenny. Just us, you and I. We're the only ones who know the truth. We share it. Just us. No one else needs to know. Just us.

'There is no us.'

How wrong you are.

'There is no us,' screamed Jenny.

You think I hadn't thought that you could turn on me? You think I haven't thought about this? You think I've left no trail to you, to here? You kill me and they will know everything about us, and more.

'What do you mean? And more?'

You like this. You like the danger. It makes you feel…

'Don't say it.'

But it does. It excites you. Why else would you do it?

'No one would believe you.'

Oh, they would. You think I haven't planned this? You think Amy Windle was the first one? Don't kid yourself. Accept it, Jenny, we are in this together. Now put the gun down, I have something new for you.

NINETEEN

The something new was body number four.

A teacher from Burnley, older than the rest but this time with no visible injuries or disturbance. Wrapped alongside her in the plastic black shroud was her handbag, spilling its usual collection of favourite touch-up cosmetics, loose sanitary products, some change, store cards, tissues, a couple of pens, one of which didn't work, no purse but a diary full of the clues Jenny needed to know the woman was a teacher, and a shopping list on a loose piece of paper torn from something other, from which you could tell she was married, or living with someone. Jenny went with living with someone. There was no ring on any significant finger, but there was a smashed smartphone, well and truly destroyed, without any way of turning it on. That was becoming a pattern. Jenny took the belongings and put them in a tin and put them with the other tins.

Body number five arrived less than a week later, but thankfully, perhaps, one of the local farmers, Peter, had called in a favour and brought over a pig with a twisted gut to dispose of. Pyre Number five would have to be built strong and high for this once magnificent specimen.

'Want a hand with it?' Peter had offered. 'He's a beast of a pig, shame really, was going to make a pretty penny out of this one. I'd mentioned him to the butchers in Skipton but now he's worth bugger all. My own fault. I can give you fifty quid for doing this.'

Jenny took the money. She said, 'Don't worry, I can manage.'

'You sure? Took three of us and a pulley and a load of rope to shift him.'

Jenny smiled. She knew who the other two would have been. The brothers, as they get called, because they are. Twins, near identical. Two giants of men who play rugby for Keighley, which had given them enough scars over the years to tell them more easily apart. When they aren't playing, they are paid farm hands. Jenny said, 'As long as I can get him into the scoop then I'm fine.'

'Well, I'll help you roll him in, least I can do.'

They had grown up together, Peter, the big farmer and Jenny.

They had been in the same class all the way through school, even since nursery. He always had a sweet smile. Jenny once sat on his chest when the whole class were playing Kiss Catch in the field behind the school. They must have been eleven, perhaps less. He said, 'Are you going to kiss me then?' It was in a way that suggested he wanted to be kissed, but at the same time he wasn't demanding to be. Jenny said, 'Nah. Why would I want to kiss you?' and ran off. Jenny had often wondered, just like so many people around here, whether Peter and her should have tried to make something more of the ease that existed between them. Perhaps then this wouldn't be her life.

'You okay these days?' said Peter after they'd rolled and scooped the dead beast of a pig. 'Don't see you much down The Rose.'

'Yeah, I'm fine, thanks. Just not comfortable in there these days.'

'Aye, Tom can be a bit of an arse. I can understand why we don't see you much. Just seems a shame. There's many of us down there that miss you. Rosie was asking about you the other night.'

'Was she?' Jenny could feel herself blushing at the speed shown of her response. Peter just smiled, knowingly and without any judgement. Jenny tried to move the conversation on, adding, 'I'll nip in soon, and say hello.'

'So, where do you get to instead? You do still get out? Can't have you staying in all the time?'

People in these parts had become sensitive about that. There was a farmer in Airton three years back who started to isolate himself. No one heard from him in a week. He was found hanging in his barn. Since then, everyone looks out for each other more often. Sometimes it's intrusive but in Jenny's eyes, when Peter, or Malcolm does it, it's kind of sweet because deep down they all know how close everyone is to it.

'You know, mainly Skipton really.'

'I heard there's a night at The Two Sisters for your — ' and embarrassed, he trailed off.

'For my sort?' Jenny said with a smile.

'You know I didn't mean it like that.'

'I know. You don't have to worry, but yes. It's nice not to be gawped at when out. Sometimes it can get a little uncomfortable knowing you're the local gossip.'

'Well, you know how it is. There's not much for people to talk about round here. It's either pigs, or sheep, or ramblers.'

'Or the lesbian running old Jim's farm.'

'You do know we refer to it as your farm?'

'About time too.'

Later that afternoon, Jenny burnt the pig, together with body number five. She still hadn't cleared away the ashes from the pyre for body number four.

TWENTY

Thursday. Market day in Skipton. Jenny had gone in for no other reason than for a change of scene and to wander the stalls.

'Hello stranger,' said Rosie, tapping Jenny on the shoulder and greeting her with the broadest of smiles. 'You not going to give me a hug?'

They hugged.

It meant more to one than the other.

'I've missed you. You've not been in for ages,' said Rosie.

'I'm sorry. I've been, been, been…'

'I know, busy. I think it's great.'

'What is?'

'That you've been coming down here.'

Jenny was confused.

'You know,' and Rosie nudged Jenny with her elbow. 'On a night out.'

'Who told you that?'

'Peter,' said Rosie, seeing the look on Jenny's face. 'Don't worry, he was discreet about it. He only told me. Seriously, I think it's great. I want my best friend to be happy. Why shouldn't you have someone? So, come on, tell us. What's it like? Met anyone yet?'

'I don't know really,' said a still uncertain Jenny. 'I've not been that often. It's not like I'm doing it to meet anyone. It's just nice not to feel the odd one out.'

'Or have my twat husband on your case?'

'Yeah, that too. Sorry. Can you forgive me?'

'For not wanting my twat husband on your case, absolutely. For not telling me, no.'

'I'll come to yours more, to make it up to you.'

'You will not. If you want to make it up to me, you can take me with you sometime.'

'You don't mean that, do you?'

'Well, not in the same way as you, but it sounds fun and if my best friend goes then why not me?'

'It can be a bit full on.'

'Even better.'

'And it's not just women.'

'So?'

'I'm just saying.'

'I'm no prude. You know that. Has anyone tried to pick you up yet? I bet they have. I bet you've got them falling over themselves. Why are you looking at me like that?'

'Do you remember…?'

'Skipton station?'

Jenny nodded.

'Of course I do. Oh, you're not saying it was me? We were kids, and you were dating thingy back then. What was his name? Didn't he have a funny ear?'

'No, of course it wasn't you. I knew before then, just don't want to admit it I guess. It was a good kiss though.'

'It was a great kiss.'

It was a confession that meant more to one than the other.

'Rosie?'

'What do you think to this one?'

Jenny paused. They'd been wandering the stalls as they spoke but now, as Rosie was contemplating the rolls of fabric on old Mrs Botham's stall, Jenny couldn't take her eyes off her friend.

'Jenny? What is it? It's not us, is it? Because I'm sorry, I'm just not...'

Jenny thought Rosie did not feel comfortable finishing her sentence, so she did it for her.

'No, it's not us, and it's okay, I know you're not.'

'It's just that I like cock too much.'

Jenny laughed, not least at the face old Mrs Botham pulled. Not one of disgust, but wistful agreement, and a dash of *I should be so lucky*.

'I don't believe I've just said that aloud — and in the middle of Skipton market.' And then, sensing Jenny and old Mrs Botham still staring at her, Rosie added, 'I mean, not that Tom's cock is lacking. It's okay but it's not like Monster's.'

'Monster's?' asked Mrs Botham.

'Now his was a cock,' laughed Rosie. 'What was his name? You remember him, don't you, Jenny? Made my eyes water. What was his name?'

Jenny playfully shrugged her shoulders.

'Oh, you do. Worse thing though, I saw him the other day, over in Keighley. I couldn't remember his name and I struggled at first to even recognise him because he's lost all his hair. He says to me, "Hello Rosie", and when it finally twigged who he was, I almost screeched, *Monster* at him. Don't laugh. It gets worse. We get chatting and it turns out he's living in Burnley and was married to a teacher, but … she went missing recently. Missing as in….' And Rosie raised her eyebrows in a prompting manner.

'As in?' said Jenny.

'As in — no one knows. She went out one night to meet the other teachers and never turned up. Can you imagine that?'

Jenny said nothing.

'Monster looked so ill. He was over in Keighley seeing her parents and obviously he's beside himself but all I could do was remember the size of his willy. I wouldn't know where to start if that happened to you, Jenny.'

Jenny didn't speak for a moment, just kept running the nearest fabric through her fingers until, with a croak in her voice, she said, 'Aren't you meant to say that about your husband? You know, if he disappeared.'

'No, that one is easy. If he disappeared we'd start by having a party, and then I'd change all the locks, empty the safe and head for Spain. You could come too. I hear they have loads of your sort of places down there.'

Jenny tried to laugh. She tried to show it meant nothing, but with a quick look at her watch, she blustered. 'Is that the time? Damn, I need to get back. Sorry, Rosie.'

'Okay, but don't be so much of a stranger, not unless you're going to then introduce me to your stunning new girlfriend who owns a brewery, or better still a vineyard in Spain.'

'I promise.'

'Seriously, Jenny. There's been other women on the news, you must have seen it. Other women going missing. Please be careful and don't be a stranger.'

They hugged and kissed again, both cheeks, and then hugged again.

Jenny didn't want to let go.

'Jenny, are you alright?' said Rosie, breaking away from Jenny's embrace.

Jenny brushed away the beginnings of a tear. Nodding, she said, 'If you see Monster again, give him my love and I hope he soon finds out what happened to his wife.'

'You make it sound like something bad has happened to her?'

'I guess these things never seem to end well, do they?'

TWENTY-ONE

'It has to stop.'

They were in Jenny's kitchen, drinking coffee. Jenny didn't want them to be there having this conversation, but she had to say what she wanted to say.

Not this again.

'I mean it.'

Didn't you say that last time.

'That teacher, from Burnley. I went to school with her husband.'

So? What does it matter?

'It's on the news. Didn't you see? They're saying there's a pattern. It's getting too dangerous.'

It's not getting dangerous enough.

'What do you mean?'

You should do the next one. I mean it. You should do it. Find them, choose them, pick them out and then separate them from whoever they're with. It's a bit like trying to get a problem sheep out of herd. You know how that goes. Do you do all that whistling and shouting come by, come by? Remember One Man And His Dog on TV? Of course, you did. It's a real skill. Must have taken you years to learn? No, I'm serious, you should do the next one. You pick them out and separate them off and I'll help you kill them. Then you can burn them. Then you'll really understand.

'I don't want to understand.'

Come on, it feels wonderful. All the planning, the waiting, watching, the working out where and how to do it. There's so many cameras around now, it's becoming an art. Come with me, you must. We'd be like Bonnie and Clyde.

'No.'

Just no?

'What else do you want me to say? No, thank you?'

That's funny, but no. Didn't mean that. You haven't sworn at me yet today?

'So?'

Just saying. I like it. I like it when you're more delicate, more womanly. Do they say that to you on your nights out? I bet you could be quite butch? You're surprisingly strong even if you don't look it. Hey, you can get one of them from there? Now

imagine that. She'll think the two of you are there to be truthful
to yourselves, but secretly you're there to find someone to kill.

'No.'

Why not?' Come on, it will be fun.

'That's too close to home.'

Is it? I don't think so.

'It's Skipton, it's on the doorstep.'

But the teacher from Burnley, that was okay? But not anyone
from Skipton? We could go to Leeds instead. There are plenty of
bars and clubs for your sort there. You never know, you might
have some fun, the other sort of fun I mean, beforehand.

'I don't want to.'

Now who's being a puritan?

Jenny didn't bother arguing. With the coffee finished, she left
the cups to be washed later.

Why not do it now?

'It gives me something to do later,' said Jenny.

Good, because I've got something for you to do now. Don't
worry, this one's only small, so you'll have no problems doing
her by yourself, only I think you'll need to get a move on. She's
been in the back of the van for over a day. I found this one in

Lancaster, or I should say a little village just outside. I've forgotten what its called. She was out jogging. Stupid girl had earphones in. Never heard a thing. I've kept the phone and a couple of other bits she had on her. I know you like keeping something of them but it's not the best of ideas. Other than that, she's naked. I wanted to have a look at her. I like them petite. I'll be back in a week's time. In the meantime, see who you can find, or shall I just go after the landlady?

TWENTY-TWO

That night the wind ran amok. In what should have been the silence of her own isolation it rampaged through every nook and cranny and branch like a hooligan drunk.

Not that Jenny never noticed. She never heard the insults, the shouting of the loose-fitting gate or the bins being used as footballs. She was lost, in her own thoughts and strange fantasies.

TWENTY-THREE

You ready?

It had been ten days, not a week. Ten days of not knowing when the call would come, not knowing what she'd be doing, not daring to tell Rosie for fear of losing her forever, not daring to not see her. Jenny went to The Rose on all but two of those nights to sit near the end of the bar, to keep Rosie in sight throughout. It took Twat Face just two nights to become vicious. Just the way he looked at Jenny was enough, and when he spoke it was either as if she wasn't there or he was spitting in her face.

How little you knew about your wife, thought Jenny, if you believe I could steal her from under you. And why not him? Why can't it be his body in one of those tarpaulins?

But now, when Jenny heard —

You ready?

She knew she wasn't, she never would be ready, not for this. But she could imagine something, she could imagine a time, she could imagine it being Twat Face.

'Does it have to be a woman?' she said.

Why? Who else you got in mind? No, don't tell me, let me guess. Twat Face? Yeah? No. Too difficult.

Instead, they went to the Two Sisters. The jeans and boots she wore on her last visit were replaced with skin-tight jeans and a spangly strappy top and this time she wore her hair down, and not in her usual ponytail with the odd wisp escaping the side.

That top, it's very similar to the one that student was wearing.

'Amy Windle?'

Yeah, her.

'So?'

It looks good on you. You look nice in it.

And then —

You best be sober. You can't do this drunk.

'And I can't do this sober.'

What about her?

In the baby blue T-shirt and tight-fitting jeans and night-out sandals.

'No,' said Jenny, 'she's only sipping her drink. She puts the straw to her lips but nothing is ever consumed.'

Clever. Nicely spotted, so what about her?

With the full brunette curves and dancing with abandonment on the makeshift dance floor.

'No.'

Okay, her?

A slender woman in an unseasonal dress and Doc Martin boots.

'Perhaps. What do I do now?'

She keeps giving you the eye. You should go and talk to her. Find out if she is by herself, or with friends. If she's with friends, it's a no. You need them alone.

'Then what about her instead?'

At the darker end of the bar, dressed down, nervous and shy, nothing special but nothing off-putting either. Definitely alone, making out like she knows what's happening, making out she is certain of herself and her sexuality whilst all the time screaming something other.

Yes. Try her, but remember —

'Yeah, I know. I heard you the first time.'

Then tell me. Tell me the golden rules.

'She's got to be here alone.'

And?

'She can't be well-known.'

Good. And?

'She can't be too drunk, but she mustn't be sober either.'

And don't draw attention to yourself. If she starts to be loud, then backoff. She mustn't be remembered, and nor must you.

TWENTY-FOUR

Three hours later Jenny was in the alleyway behind the castle in a breathless and hopeless embrace with the woman from the dark end of the bar, hands in each other's hair and over clothes, veering between their shared want for this moment and the many crises of belief.

I can't

I can

I want

But what if

But it's been so long since

I felt this free

And understood

And wanted,

Loved

Or as close to it as lust allows.

'Where do you live?' said the woman from the dark end of the bar.

Don't tell her.

Golden rule. Don't tell her.

'Miles away' Jenny said.

It was the same answer Jenny had given three times already that night, but for the first time the woman looked disappointed.

'You?' asked Jenny.

'Coniston,' the woman said. 'You know it?'

'Yeah. But I've never seen you around there. I go through it a lot.'

What have you done? You're telling her too much. You hear me? Can you hear me? You're telling her too much.

'I just moved there,' the woman said. 'Only place around here I could afford.'

Too much. This is not the plan.

'Where were you before?' asked Jenny.

This is not how it's done.

'Here in Skipton, but I got divorced. Well, I'm getting divorced.'

Why didn't you find all this out earlier? You should have found this out.

'Are you okay?' the woman said.

'Yeah, very okay.'

'Just seemed you —'

She knows. Fuck, she knows. Concentrate. You're fucking up.

Thought you didn't swear.

'Just seemed you, like you disappeared,' said the woman.

'Disappeared?'

'Yeah, like you suddenly weren't here?'

'There's nowhere I'd rather be.'

Too late. She's worried. Look at her. She knows something is wrong. Time to walk away. It will be too much of a struggle. You're not ready for the fight. Trust me, you don't have it in you.

'You could —'

Could what, Jennifer? Come on, what? What are you going to say?

'You could invite me back to yours.'

What the FUCK!

'I don't think I'm ready for that. Not straight away.'

Thank fuck for that. See, what did I tell you? You have to listen to me.

'I understand. Sorry,' said Jenny.

'No, it's me,' said the woman, struggling not to apologise.

Hah, that old chestnut.

Shut the fuck up.

'It's just that you're the first person I've kissed since him. You're the first person I've wanted to kiss since. But it's all so sudden. I was just curious tonight, that's why I went.'

Utter rubbish, I bet you she's been watching girl on girl porn for months.

'Sssssh. It's okay,' said Jenny. 'I understand. I'm not usually like this either.'

'Really? You seem so much more confident.'

'I think it's called relief.'

'But you said it wasn't your first time there.'

'It wasn't, but it's my first time behind the castle.'

They both laughed and then tried to stifle their laughter so they would not be heard.

The woman said, 'I couldn't think of anywhere else to go.'

'Better than down by the canal,' giggled Jenny.

Oh, for crying out loud, say your goodbyes and we can try somewhere else, you never know.

'I'd like to see you again.'

'I'd like that too.'

'How about the weekend?'

Don't get sucked in.

'The weekend would be good,' said Jenny, and added, 'How you getting home?'

'Taxi. You?'

'Me too. I've got to go past Coniston. How about we share a cab? I'll be paying to go that way.'

'I thought you were miles away.'

'If Malham is miles away then yes.'

What the fuck are you doing? Just tell her your little secret and have done with it? Hey sweetie, I burn bodies for cash and I'd like to burn yours too.

'I thought I'd seen you before. It's a small world.'

Fuck fuck fuck, fuck.

TWENTY-FIVE

Back in Jenny's kitchen in the early hours of the morning.

Well, I hope you're pleased with yourself.

'Yes, actually, I am. She's nice. I like her.'

That's not what we agreed for tonight.

'You told me to go talk to her.'

But not for that reason. What was that anyway. Fuck me.

'Stop swearing, You don't like me doing it so you shouldn't either.'

Fuck you, wasting my evening. It would have been better if I'd gone out alone. Jesus wept.

'Maybe I don't want to do it anymore.'

Oh, I get it. One quick fumble down a dark alley and you're in love. It was not what we agreed.

'Not everything has to go your way. Somethings are my choice.'

No, they're not. They never have been, and they never will. What I say goes. I know what I'm doing. You're just a stupid girl and that's all you've ever been. Fuck me, kisses behind the castle? Next you'll be straightening your hair. Thank fuck she didn't show you her knickers. You can't see her again.

'I will if I want to.'

And you don't want to.

'It's not your decision.'

Want a bet.

'I need to go to bed. It's late.'

And what about me?

'What about you?'

You've had your fun.

'I've no idea what you're saying. You're not suggesting…?'

Of course not. Fuck, it's like you don't know me.

'It's late, just go to sleep. You can sleep on the couch. There'll be no one around at this time of night.'

You owe me. Maybe it's time for Rosie of The Rose?

'Don't you dare. We talked about this.'

No. You talked about this. I said nothing.

'Don't you threaten me or her.'

Or?

'I'm warning you.'

Or?

'Don't you dare.'

Or?

'Don't you fucking dare.'

TWENTY-SIX

The next morning Jenny had to wait to ring The Rose.

Twat Face answered.

'Is Rosie there?'

'Yes. Why?'

'I need to speak to her.'

'She's busy at the moment.'

'I need to speak to her. It's urgent.'

'And I said, she's busy at the moment.'

'For once in your life stop being a twat and put her on the phone.'

'For once in your life stop trying to live your life through my wife.'

'Put her on the phone or I'll come down there and cut off your balls and feed them to you. Fuck knows it will taste better than the slop you serve as food.'

'Don't you fucking dare talk to me like that, you stupid little —'

Jenny heard some muffled words, some argued words and then, 'Give me the phone.' It was Rosie, 'Jenny? Jenny? What is it?'

Jenny hadn't thought past Rosie being there.

'Jenny?'

Think, think quick.

Quicker.

'Rosie, are you okay?'

'Of course I am, Jenny.'

'Only I had this dream. A really bad dream. It was so vivid, and you were in it. I guess, I guess I panicked.'

'Jenny, I'm fine. It's you I should be worried about.'

'Why? Why you worrying about me? It was only a dream. I'm sorry. I shouldn't have panicked. I shouldn't have called.'

'Have you not seen the news?'

'No. I've not had it on.'

'You know what I mentioned when I saw you in Skipton. About Monster, and his wife and how women keep disappearing and the police think there's a pattern? Well, a woman was attacked, in Coniston, last night, in her own home whilst she was asleep.'

'Jesus, what happened to her?'

'She fought them off, but they made a right mess of her face apparently. They are saying it might be linked.'

'Have they said who she is? This woman?'

As if you don't know.

'They've not released her name. They only said she was in her thirties and had been out in Skipton the night before. The only thing on in Skipton last night was, well you know where.'

'Where is she now?'

'Skipton Infirmary, I guess. Jenny, is there something you're not telling me.'

'No. It's all good. I was just thinking I might know her, but I don't. Look, sorry, I've got to go.'

'Why don't I pop over later? The delivery is due anytime now, so after that? Don't worry if you're up on the fields. I'll call you when I get to the farm.'

'No. I promise, everything's okay. Thanks. Sorry just got a busy day.'

Dropping the phone, Jenny ran to the kitchen sink and vomited over the dishes left there from the night before. Her stomach pulsed, her eyes streamed, she gripped tight to the side of the sink to stop herself sliding to the floor.

'What have you done?'

What have I done?

'You heard me.'

Don't take that tone with me. I told you what would happen. I told you.

'What did you do?'

You know what I did.

'But she was... '

She was what? I'll tell you what she was, she was a fucking bitch. And I told you she'd fight. Fucker was a right scratcher and then started screaming. I knew it. I told you. Didn't I tell you.

'You said not to go back to her.'

I said you shouldn't. I knew I should have done it by myself.

'We're in the news now. Haven't you heard?'

We've been in the news for months. Nothing to worry about now.

'But none of the others got away?'

That you know of.

'You mean there's been more? How many more?'

Are you telling me you really don't know?

'I thought this was just an every-so-often thing.'

Every so often? Fuck that. I love it. Every single second of it.

'You're sick.'

I'm sick? Listen to you. You're no different to me. All this danger. You could have put a stop to it that first night but no, you kept going. You've even got keepsakes from each of them. Fucking keepsakes. Christ, listen to me. I'm turning into you with all this swearing. Now get your boots on, I've got something for you.

'What?'

You heard.

'When? When did you have the time?'

Easy, first thing this morning. I've been watching the local school. Had my eye on one of the mums but I was there early looking for cameras, turns out one of the teachers opens up way before anyone else arrives and then goes for a run. Got her on one of the back roads up there, near where you got that student.'

'Amy Windle?'

Yeah, her. You did me a favour that night, you do know that, don't you? She got away from me and I was struggling to catch up with her. She was fast. You ploughing into her, It was like all my Christmas' had come at once. She wasn't dead, you know, not after you hit her. What's that face for? You liked her, didn't you? She was a bit like that one last night. You fall in love too easy, that's what's wrong with you.

'We have to stop.'

Oh, Jennifer, we both know that's never going to happen. You're too scared to lose the farm, and to lose Rosie, although god knows why. You do know she's been with that tart who works with her behind the bar.

Jenny didn't know what to say. Her lips moved but her disbelief was silent.

You didn't know? That's priceless. You must be the only one who didn't know. It's not that she doesn't like women, it's just that she doesn't like you.

'Shut up.'

She was going to The Two Sisters before you even knew it existed. Little old Jenny, Jenny in the closet, Jenny without the courage to admit she never wanted this damned farm. She

*never wanted to be living miles from anywhere, she never
wanted to be a lesbian, she just never had the balls to do
anything, to go anywhere. You never even had the balls to hold
a pair of balls.*

'Fuck you. Fuck you.'

*You wish. You might have something to boast about then,
something to give you some true courage instead of just frigging
yourself off in fantasies every night. Christ, and to think you
met a real nice lass last night. She was sweet, and keen on you.
You could have gone at a speed that suited you both but instead
you got angry because she wouldn't jump straight into bed with
you. Last night was nothing to do with me. Don't go blaming
me, silly little shy Jenny. Last night was all your fault. Imagine
if you could've been there at the same time as me. She wouldn't
be a problem to us now. She should be in the back of the van
instead of the young teacher, and you know that teacher well.
That's going to shake you up, when it's time to take her
keepsakes. No need to worry about that, Little Jenny. I've done
it for you. Here you go. One watch, one gold necklace, a lock of
her hair, and her wedding and engagement rings. You put all
those in one of your precious little jars so you can rub yourself
off over her later. Fuck me, your hypocrisy sickens me.*

TWENTY-SEVEN

The body was dumped as the bodies normally are.

Without ceremony in the middle of the yard.

Except this time there was no tarpaulin, just the ragged once life.

This time, I want to see her burn. Thanks to you and your sensibilities I've been depriving myself of that pleasure for months. I'll be back later. Best be ready for me, sweet shy Jenny.

TWENTY-EIGHT

Life is full of simple decisions.

Or at least you think it is. Like, whether you enjoy your meat clean, or you'll devour anything, like whether you let anger steal the space that exists between logic and your actions, or do you squeal like an angry pig or be calm and quiet and composed. Like whether you listen to the voices in your head or choose not to.

Finally alone, Jenny didn't move from her spot beside the body. Then, without any demonstration, some would say without emotion, she turned, fetched the scoop and moved the body to the cold store where she prepared it for burning before building the pyre.

She saved the teacher's keepsakes in a jar just like the others, each now named with black letters written on white labels, and the date of the body, if not the death.

But this time, she didn't put the jar back on the shelf. This time she left it in the cold store, on the marble slab, and she went back for all the others from the cellar. She lined them up alongside each other, like a collection of confessions.

An hour before she was due to burn the body she loaded the shot gun with two cartridges, she put two others in her jacket pocket, and made two phone calls. The first was anonymous, to the Skipton police. She said, 'I know who attacked the woman last night. Come to the Far Farm, Otterburn, in one hour. They'll be on the far hill above the meadow.' She cut the call off after that.

Then she rang Rosie. She wasn't answering; instead, there was a recording, it said leave a message.

'Hi, Rosie,' Jenny said, before losing herself in a long pause. When she started to speak, she stumbled through the sentence. 'I've done something really stupid. I'm sorry.' Then another long pause. And a deep audible breath. 'And I'm sorry I never had the courage to tell you I loved you. I just wish you knew sooner. I'm sorry. So very sorry.' She cut the call off straight after that.

Then Jenny busied herself, whilst keeping a constant watch on the wall of her kitchen until it was time. She left the dogs locked in the kitchen and took the Defender up to the pyre and waited. She wasn't long alone.

It's nice up here on days like this. Suns out, little bit of cloud.

'Do you want to light it?' asked Jenny.

What, no small talk? Yeah, I think I'll light it. What do you use?

'A match, and petrol, so don't get too close.'

Even with those words of guidance, the initial burst of flame came as a surprise and made them jump back.

You're right, it does smell like pork. Petrol marinated pork, weird that.

'It's because we're unclean meat.'

You comparing us to pigs? Because pigs eat anything?

'And everything.'

Does it make a difference, you know, depending on who it is? If they are young, or old, or…do they smell different?

'No. We all burn the same.'

Because we're all unclean in one way or another.

'I don't think it's that scientific.'

After watching for a while in silence

Well, I best get going.

'Why don't you wait and see it out?' said Jenny. 'When the pyre collapses in on itself, it's a special moment. It's like a soul is released.'

Okay, but you make it sound like a load of hippy shit.

They waited, and despite the increasingly overcast sky the heat from the pyre was sufficient to keep them standing some feet away.

By the way, why the shotgun?

'I always come up to the fields with it.'

Is it loaded?

'Always is when I'm up here. Had too many dogs and the like frightening the sheep.'

So, it's not for me then?

'It's a just-in-case thing.'

Just in case what?

They heard a car arriving down at the farm and very soon after Jenny's phone rang.

Who's that?

Jenny looked at the screen of her phone, and without answering the phone, said, 'Rosie'

What's she doing here?

'She's worried about me.'

You best answer it then. I don't think you want her up here with us.

Jenny put the phone to her ear. 'Hi. No, you stay there. I'm over by the far side of the meadow. I'll be down soon. Why not go in the kitchen, the doors open but don't let Meg and Jess out. I've left them there. Yeah, the far side of the meadow. And I can see you too. Yeah, always another sheep, bloody ramblers with their dogs again.'

As they were talking two police cars arrived and three offices stepped out.

'Yeah, don't worry, Rosie, I called them earlier. They can come up here if they want but I'd prefer it if you didn't. I'll be down very soon.'

Jenny hung up.

What the fuck are the police doing here?

'I called them.'

So, they can watch you burn another body?

'We're not burning another body. It's a pig in there.'

A pig? So, where's the body I dropped off this morning.

'In the cold store. Enough is enough.'

What have you told them?

'That if they come here now they'd find who attacked the woman from Coniston last night.'

You stupid bitch. How many of them are here?

'I don't know.'

You do know. That cow from the pub told you.

'Don't come any closer.'

Jenny cocked the gun.

Is that it? You think by turning me in you'll get off?

'No. I know what will happen to me, but this way I can stop you.'

You think it's that easy?

'There's only one way in and out of the farm, and that's the yard.'

Or there's over the tops here, I could take the Defender. There's enough tracks.

'You don't know these hills. You won't get far.'

I know them better than you think now put the bloody gun down and give me the keys.

'No.'

Do as you're told, just as you have been doing all your life.

'No. No more. It's over now.'

Down in the yard the police were getting directions to the far side of the meadow from Rosie. She said, 'If you go to that gate there, you can see them on the hill. She said she should be down very soon.'

Rosie led them to the gate, and from there they could see Jenny.

'She's got a shotgun,' said one of the policemen, peering into the distance.

Rosie said, 'She's a farmer, they all have.'

'Why is she standing by a bonfire?'

'I shouldn't tell you this, but she burns the sheep when they die. We get a lot of walkers who let the dogs off the lead up here and they worry the sheep.'

'Is that how they should dispose of them?'

'Not really. Just easier I think.'

Then there was the realisation. It quickened their tone.

'Is she pointing the gun at herself? She is. She's pointing it at herself. I thought you said she was alone up there?'

'I thought she was. She didn't say otherwise.'

'Looks like she's having a right argument with someone, but I can't see anyone up there with her. I can only see her?'

Back on the hillside.

Put the fucking gun down

'No. I told you, it ends here.'

I decide when it ends, not you, and it's not now. So, give me the gun and the keys.

'No.'

Then you're going to have to shoot me because there's no way I'm going to be handed in like this.

'Don't think I won't.'

It's the end of both of us if you keep this up.

'I don't care. It's gone on long enough.'

TWENTY-NINE

The police opened the gate and started walking towards the meadow. Rosie walked with them.

'You got a mobile number for her?'

'Yes,' said Rosie.

'Pass it here. Let us call her.'

It rings until —

'Jenny?' Says the policeman on the phone. 'Is that you, Jenny?'

'Yes.'

'Jenny, are you alone up there? We can hear an argument but can't see anyone else up there? Is there anyone up there with you?'

Tell him to fuck off and hang the phone up. If we run together, we can get away.

'Shut the fuck up

'Jenny, what did you just say?'

'Nothing. I wasn't talking to you.'

'Jenny, your friend, Rosie, is here too. We're coming up. You will put the gun down, won't you?'

'I can't.'

'Why not Jenny?'

Because I'll fucking steal it and shoot the lot of you. This is madness, Jenny. We can still get away.

'Jenny, why not? We're here to help you, Jenny, but we can't help you if you've got a shot gun in your hands.'

'It has to stop.'

'What has? Jenny, what has got to stop?'

'The killing.'

'What killing, Jenny? The killing of the sheep?'

'The women.'

'What women, Jenny?'

'All of them.'

Give me the gun.

'I don't know what you mean, Jenny.'

'One of you needs to look in the cold store. Then you'll know what I mean.'

From up on the hill Jenny watched as one of the police officers split off from the rest, and taking Rosie with them, headed back to the yard, and to the cold store.

Oh, what the fuck have you done? You've moved the keepsakes? You've put them in with the body? You stupid bitch. I should have killed you when I had the chance. Should have done it when we first met. Now give me the fucking gun.

'Stop shouting at me

'Jenny? Jenny, no one is shouting at you? We're just chatting, on the phone, please don't put the phone down, let's just keep talking.'

Give me the gun.

'Get your hands off it

'Jenny, whatever's happening we can sort it. I just need you to put the gun down and tell me if there is anyone else with you?'

Tell them to fuck off. Now give me the gun, Jennifer.

'Stop calling me that. My name's Jenny.'

Your name's Jennifer. That's what Mum called you, it's what we all called you.

'Dad didn't. He always called me Jenny.'

Is that what this is about?

'Jenny,' said the police officer, 'we can't see anyone else up there. Is there anyone? Are they behind the bonfire? Are they behind the Defender? Jenny please tell us.'

'I'll shoot.'

'Jenny, whatever you do, don't shoot. We won't come any closer. Is that what's worrying you? Jenny look at us, see we stopped walking. Is there anyone else there with you?'

You haven't got the balls.

'I'll do it.'

'Shit, she's dropped the phone. Quick, we need to get back' said the police officer who had been talking on the phone. 'We're too close here.'

You fucking won't. I've had enough of this. I'm going over the tops, shoot me if you want but I'm not stopping for this.

'Stay where you are.'

No fucking way. Haven't you worked this out yet? This is it, this is the choice. It's not just me, or just you; it's us, together. We're the same. They get me, they get you. They get you, they get me. But I don't care about you. Never have done. Fuck me, you've been hard work all your life. You should have run off, got away from this godforsaken place when you had the chance.

'Like you did.'

Yeah, like I did. You can't blame me, I never wanted to live here. I never wanted the farm. I was never like you. You were always daddy's golden girl. Helping him all the time, with the lambing and the fencing. Going to bloody country shows with him. You should've skipped off to Leeds station like you said you were going to do and fucked right off, found out what life had to offer you, instead of sitting daydreaming amongst those bloody sheep. You've been a burden to me all along.

'Stop it. Stop it, stop talking.'

Why?

'It's not true.'

Isn't it? So, why are you so angry with me?

'Because you left us. You left me.'

I never had a choice. What would have happened had I stayed? We would have shared the farm? There was no chance of that happening. Father knew I didn't care for the place. You should have known too. For fucks sake I told you enough times. Now give me the gun.

'No.'

Give me the gun.

'Let go of it.'

Give it me.

'Let go.'

Give me the gun.

Jenny pushed the barrel of the shot gun under her chin. A policeman shouted 'Jenny.'

She didn't hear.

You don't have what it takes. Believe me I know. We both know. I even sent you a plane ticket. You could have joined me. You didn't even have the guts to come for a holiday. Father knew what would have happened if you did.

'I will. I'll shoot.'

Go on then. Do it. Do it. See how I care.

'It'll be the end of us both.'

Hallelujah, at long last, I'll be free of you.

'You always were free of me. You never came back, not even for mum and dad's funerals.'

Christ, you sound just like the younger brat you always were. I didn't come back because I was already dead.

'You could have stayed.'

In this shit hole? Why would I? I never wanted this life. You knew that. They knew that. Why do you think Dad and me fought so much? This place was so bloody precious to him. No one could change a thing whilst he was alive. Didn't you want to redecorate the farmhouse once? You did, I remember. He wouldn't even let you do that. He just wanted us to run around him, fetching and carrying like his fucking dogs. You're still no different.

'You could have survived. You could have got better.'

If I had stayed here? Oh, Jenny, you're so fucking naive. You don't survive what I had. If they couldn't cure me in America, they certainly couldn't cure me here.

'You were my sister.'

So?

'You abandoned me to this place.'

That was nothing to do with me. And I didn't abandon you. I moved on. Can you not see? I had someone. I had a life. I didn't want...this. I wanted something else and I found it. Might not have lasted long, but at least I had it.

'The first chance you got you were gone.'

It's exactly what you should have done, now give me the gun.

'Stay back. I'll do it.'

For fuck's sake please do. Release us both. Here, let me help you.

THIRTY

The single shot echoed off the meadow hillside. With nothing to contain it, it rang out over the deserted hills until it became another empty gesture. A handful of sheep bolted, for a few yards at least, then went back to their grazing.

A single body fell, half in the fire, half on the grass.

There were no more murders.

At least, not by Jenny.

Because it's good to know what happens next

EPILOGUE

Whenever spring comes, farmers watch, watch with caution.

We watch the flock, we watch the weather.

We watch the prices demanded at the markets and the wholesalers.

We watch the politicians, and for walkers and their dogs.

We watch the sunrises, we watch the sunsets

And we watch each other.

We watch for breaking ranks,

We watch for disease.

We watch for poachers.

And we watch what the bastard neighbours we've angered in the past are saying.

We watch for vets visiting other farms

We make excuses for them visiting our own.

We spend our lives watching and making sure things don't die.

Until they should die.

Until we die.

And then those around us watch us,

Just for a while...

Then everyone gets on with their lives

End

The Without Whom Gallery

Always, Alex, Harriet, Gill, and my mother, for all your love, inspiration, and

support. My friends, for your love and support and regular prodding.

Especially, Leo, my Italian taskmaster, Steve, my Barnsley superhero, and

Bill, my mentor-man, and Lisa, Matt, and Letty, Joe, and Peter, for

encouraging me to dream.